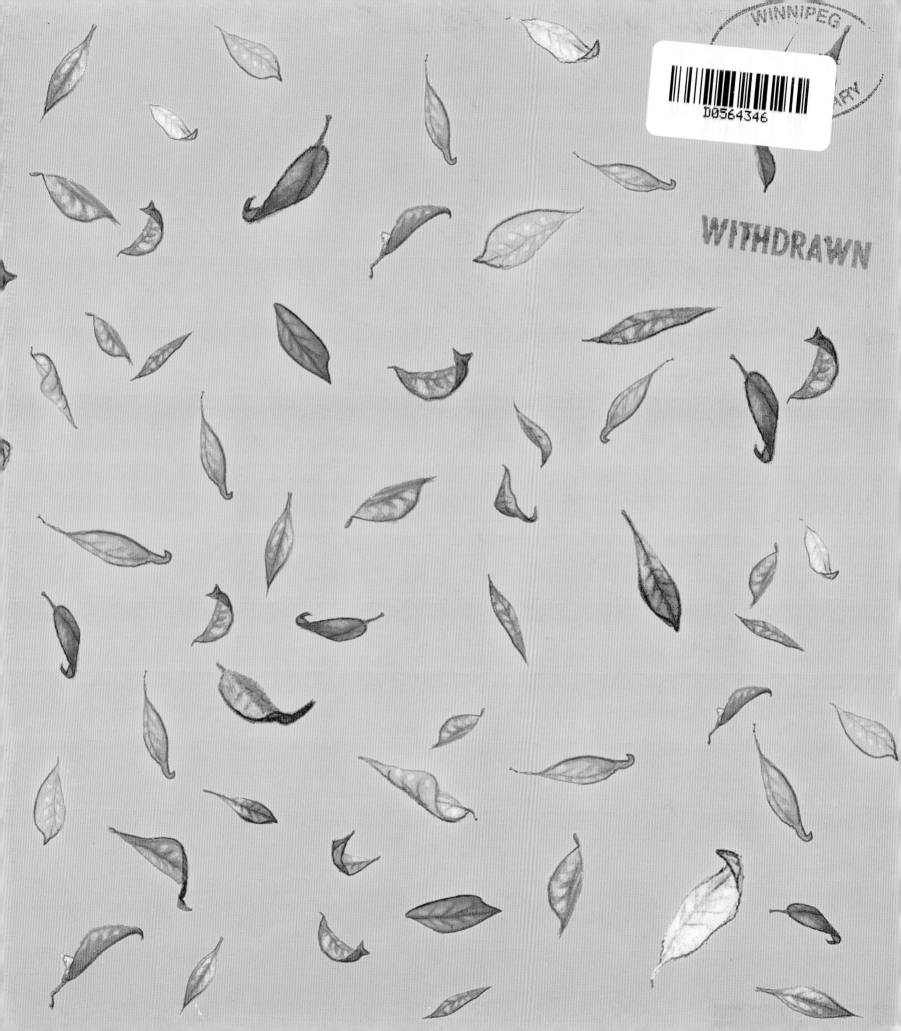

for Felix

C.F.

PUFFIN BOOKS

Published by the Penguin Group: London, New York, Ireland,
Australia, Canada, India, New Zealand and South Africa
Penguin Books Ltd, Registered Offices:
80 Strand, London WC2R 0RL, England

www.penguin.com

First published 2006
1 3 5 7 9 10 8 6 4 2
Text copyright © Sam McBratney, 2006
Illustrations copyright © Charles Fuge, 2006
The moral right of the author and illustrator has been asserted
Manufactured in China
ISBN 13: 978-0-141-38082-7
ISBN 10: 0-141-38082-9

Yes We Can!

Sam McBratney & Charles Fuge

PUFFIN

Little Roo was chasing leaves one windy day.
Roo's friends, Country Mouse
and Quacker Duck, were waiting
to play with him.

"Let's make a big pile of leaves," said Roo.
"A mountain of leaves," said Country Mouse.
"The biggest ever seen!" quacked Duck.

They began to collect up all the leaves they could find
but making a leaf mountain is hard work,
so after a while they stopped for a rest.

While they were resting, Little Roo
said to his friend Quacker Duck,
"I know something you can't do.
You can't jump over a big, big log."

"Yes I can,"

said Quacker Duck.

Quacker Duck tried as hard
as she could,
but little ducks aren't
made to jump over
big, big logs.

Country Mouse thought it was
so funny when Quacker Duck
fell over the fallen-down tree.

"Don't you **laugh** at me!" said Quacker Duck to Country Mouse. "I know something you can't do. You can't **float** on a **puddle**."

"**Yes I can,**" said Country Mouse.

So Country Mouse tried to float
on the puddle...

but a wee mouse isn't
really made for
f l o a t i n g.

Little Roo thought it was **so** funny
when Country Mouse crawled out of the water,
soaking wet
and dripping.

"Don't you **laugh** at me!"
said Country Mouse.
"I know something you can't do.
You can't **catch** your own tail."

"**Yes I can,**"

said Roo.

Roo tried as hard as he could
to catch his own tail,
but his tail would not
be caught.

It was too far away.

Country Mouse
and Quacker Duck
laughed and laughed
as Roo ran round
in circles.

"Don't you **dare** laugh at me!" cried Roo.
"Well, **you** laughed at me!" said Mouse.
"And **you** laughed at me!" said Duck.

No one
was
happy.

No one was happy because each
had made fun of someone else
and someone else had made fun of them.

Instead of making the biggest mountain
of leaves that anyone had ever seen, they
looked as if they might all go home in a

bad mood.

Little Roo's mother came over
to see what the fuss was about.
"I'm not surprised the three of
you look so grumpy," she said.
"Nobody likes to be
laughed at!"

It was true.
No one likes to be laughed at.
"Why don't you show each other
what you **can** do?" said Roo's mum.

Roo cried, "I can jump over a big, big log!"

He hopped **up** and **over** the fallen-down tree in a jiffy.

"That's **really** good **jumping**,"
the others said.

"I can **float** on a puddle," said Quacker Duck,
taking to the water with ease.

"That's **really** excellent **floating!**"
the others agreed.

And when Country Mouse caught his own tail,
Little Roo and Quacker Duck
thought that his
tail-catching was
the best they had
ever seen.

"There now," said Roo's mother,
    "can we all be friends again?"
Little Roo, Country Mouse and
    Quacker Duck looked at one another.
They were all thinking the same thing . . .

"Yes
we
can!"

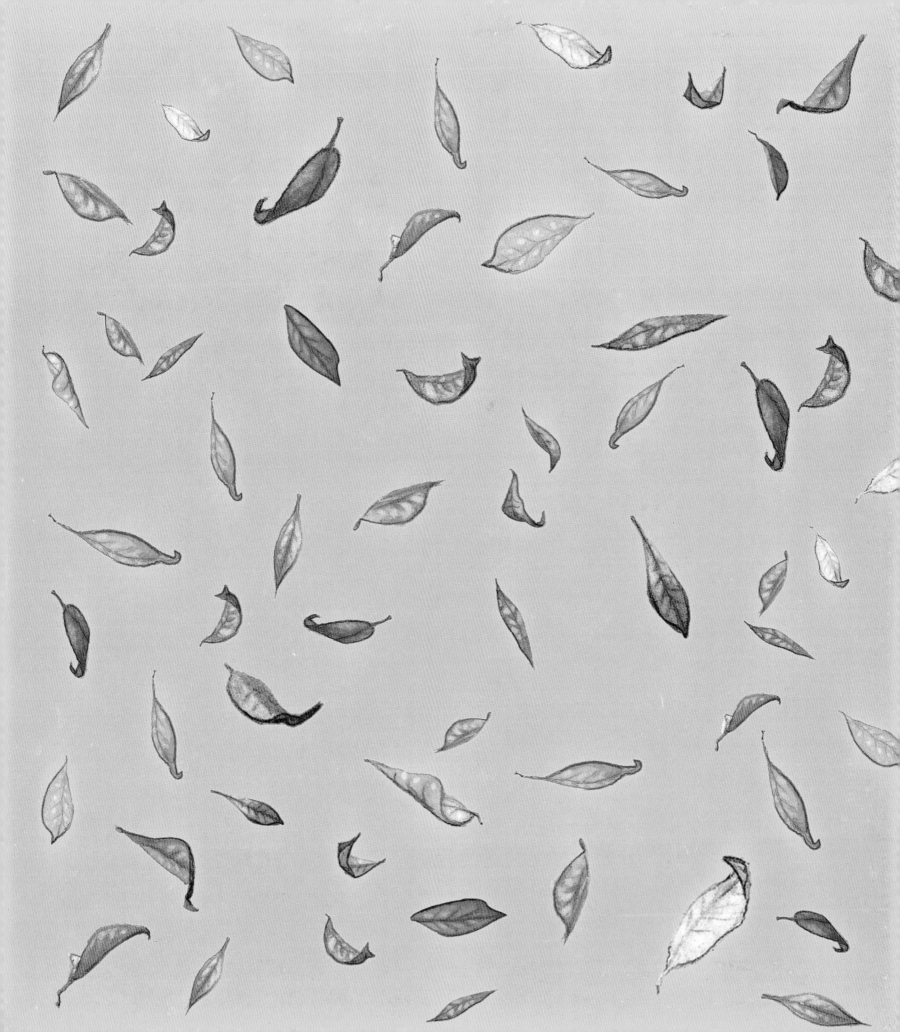